# THE SEVEN AND THE UFOS

Enjoy another thrilling adventure with the Secret Seven. They are Peter, Janet, Pam, Colin, George, Jack, Barbara and, of course, Scamper the spaniel.

When Jack's annoying sister, Susie, claims to have seen an unidentified flying object, the Secret Seven are almost sure she's making it up. But she's not the only one who claims to have seen one; all over the country sightings have been reported, and it's not long before the Seven themselves see something startling coming down from the sky. What *is* going on? The Secret Seven are determined to find out!

# The Seven and the UFOs

A new adventure of the
characters created by
Enid Blyton, told by Evelyne
Lallemand, translated by
Anthea Bell

*Illustrated by Maureen Bradley*

**KNIGHT BOOKS**
Hodder and Stoughton

Copyright © Librairie Hachette 1979
First published in France as *Les Sept et les soucoupes volantes*

English language translation copyright © Hodder & Stoughton Ltd. 1986
Illustrations copyright © Hodder & Stoughton Ltd. 1986

First published in Great Britain by Knight Books 1986
*Third impression 1987*

**British Library C.I.P.**

Lallemand, Evelyne
   The seven and the ufos: a new adventure of the characters created by Enid Blyton.
   I. Title   II. Bradley, Maureen
   III. Les sept et les soucoupes volantes. *English*
843'.914[J]      PZ7
   ISBN 0-340-37840-9

Printed and bound in Great Britain for Hodder and Stoughton Paperbacks, a division of Hodder and Stoughton Ltd., Mill Road, Dunton Green, Sevenoaks, Kent TN13 2YA (Editorial Office: 47 Bedford Square, London WC1B 3DP) by Richard Clay Ltd., Bungay, Suffolk.

# CONTENTS

*Chapter One*

# UNIDENTIFIED FLYING OBJECTS

It was four o'clock in the afternoon, and Jack, Colin, George, Pam and Barbara had come to tea with their friends Peter and Janet. The whole Secret Seven Society was gathered in the living-room of Old Mill House.

'I don't expect tea will be long,' said Peter. 'Let's see if there's anything on television while we wait, shall we?'

He switched on the television set. The picture flickered for a moment as it came on, and then it steadied. There was a newsreader on the screen, saying, 'This is an important news flash!'

'Goodness!' said Peter. 'I wonder what's happened?'

The newsreader was looking rather serious as he began reading his bulletin. He *sounded* serious too.

'Good afternoon,' he said. 'As you may have heard earlier, an extraordinary number of sightings of unidentified flying objects has been reported all over the country since quite early this morning. We have just received news of several such U.F.O.s, or flying saucers, as they are sometimes known, being spotted over London. Reports of similar sightings have been coming in all day from the South Coast, East Anglia, the West Country, and the Midlands.'

Janet was looking frightened. 'Is the end of the world coming?' she asked in a scared little voice. She couldn't look away from the screen.

'All the newspapers are full of these remarkable events,' the newsreader went on. 'Most regional evening papers have published special supplements with accounts of the local sightings. Unfortunately, the U.F.O.s have proved difficult to photograph, and so . . .'

'I saw a poster for *our* local paper, saying "SPECIAL: U.F.O. sightings",' said Jack. 'That was on my way here, Peter — but I didn't realise what it was all about!'

'Yes, I saw that poster too,' said George.

Peter shushed them. 'Listen!' he said. 'Let's find out if there's any more.'

But the newsreader was just saying, 'And this is the end of the news flash.'

'You'd think the police would be chasing about after flying saucers, wouldn't you?' said Colin.

'And the Army!' said Pam. 'But nobody seems to be *doing* anything about it!'

'I expect they're all too scared,' said Janet, fiddling nervously with her hair. 'I'm sure *I* would be!'

'I bet it's just a fake,' said Barbara. 'Don't worry, Janet. It sounds to me like reporters trying to make a

8

big story out of nothing! Didn't you hear the news-reader say there weren't any good photographs? Well, that'll be because it's easy enough to spot a faked photograph – and the flying saucer in it usually turns out to be the hub cap of a car's wheel, or a part of a table lamp, or something like that!'

'Barbara's right,' said Peter. He got up and switched the television off. 'Come on, everyone, no point in sitting about here doing nothing! Let's go and tidy up the garden shed till tea's ready!'

The Seven went out of the living-room – but they didn't get to the shed just yet, because there was a delicious smell coming from the kitchen, and they couldn't help looking in to see what it was. Floury brown scones just coming out of the oven!

'Hallo – you're just in time!' said Peter's mother, as the children came into the kitchen. She was moving a sponge cake off her cake rack to make room for the scones. 'These don't want to wait!'

'Ooh, is all that for us?' asked Peter.

'Well, of course it's for you!' she said. 'You asked the Seven to tea, didn't you? And I know you've all got good appetites! I'm just going to split this sponge and fill it with jam – sit down and have some scones! There's butter, and honey, or last year's blackberry jelly if you'd rather.'

What a feast! The children sat down at the kitchen table and tucked in. The scones were lovely, all warm and fresh from the oven, and the cake, when it was ready, was delicious too. Scamper thought *he* ought to get a slice, and he jumped up on the kitchen stool and put his front paws on the table, panting hopefully.

'Good boy, Scamper!' Janet told him. 'Yes, of course you can have a slice of cake – can't he, Mummy?'

'Well, as I was saying, we've asked the Seven to tea, and Scamper *is* an honorary member of the Society, so I can't really say no!' said her mother, laughing.

Scamper enjoyed his cake so much that he kept looking for more, even when the whole sponge had been eaten up, and the children had to drag him out of the kitchen when they had finished their tea and were going to the garden shed.

'You know, it wouldn't hurt you to take a bit of exercise!' Peter told the dog, as they went into the shed.

'Yes, you don't want to get fat!' Colin agreed, patting Scamper's tummy. It *was* a bit fat.

'*We* could do with some exercise too, if you ask me,' said Jack. '*Mental* exercise, I mean. It must be weeks and weeks since the Secret Seven had a good mystery!'

'Not since the summer holidays,' said Pam. 'We couldn't get out and about much at Christmas because of all the snow.'

'And it was freezing at half-term in February, too,' said Barbara.

'Well, it's a fine spring day now!' said George smiling. 'And we've got a fortnight off school, so I think we ought to make the best of it!'

'Going on a flying-saucer hunt, are you?' Colin teased him. 'With pink and blue butterfly nets, I suppose!'

'It's all very well making jokes,' said Peter, 'but what would you feel like if you *really* found yourself face to face with a U.F.O.?'

'Oh, do stop talking about U.F.O.s!' said Barbara. 'I'm getting sick of the subject. I'm sure there's no such thing!'

Suddenly there were three loud knocks on the door of the garden shed. Peter signed to everyone to stop talking. This was the Secret Seven's special meeting place, and they didn't want anyone barging in! Even Scamper fell silent and pricked up his ears.

A moment later the three knocks came again.

'Who's there?' called Peter.

'It's us!' said a scared little voice.

'Oh no!' said Jack. 'It's my wretched sister Susie and her silly friend Binkie! What a cheek! Trying to get into *our* shed!'

'Oh, please, please open the door!' begged Susie.

'Nothing doing!' Peter told her firmly. 'You know very well you two don't belong to the Secret Seven, and you can't come into our shed! You don't know the password, anyway!'

'We're frightened!' wept Binkie, and she *did* sound frightened.

'Stop fooling about!' said Jack. He always felt particularly bad about Susie, because she was *his* sister and was always making a nuisance of herself to *his* friends.

'Susie's not feeling well – oh, do help us!' sobbed Binkie.

'It's just another of their tricks to get into one of our meetings!' said Barbara in a furious whisper.

'Well, it won't work,' said Jack. 'Try something a bit more convincing!' he shouted to the two little girls outside the door.

But nobody replied. There was complete silence. The Seven exchanged glances of surprise as they listened for any noises. What *was* going on, on the other side of that door?

Suddenly Scamper jumped up at the latch, several times, as if he were trying to get at the key and open the door. Peter ordered him to stop.

'Take it easy, Scamper!' he said. 'That'll do!'

He pushed the dog down, and suddenly opened the door. How surprised he was to see Susie and Binkie kneeling outside, clinging to each other, with tears running down their cheeks.

'We've just seen one!' gasped Binkie, trying to support Susie, who certainly didn't *look* well. 'It was whistling, really loud, and there was lots and lots of horrible smoke, and –'

'What smoke?' asked Peter, helping Susie up. 'What was whistling? What exactly did you see?'

Binkie stopped babbling, looked at the Seven in front of her one by one, as if she couldn't believe they were really there, and then she whispered, 'A flying saucer! That's what we saw, a flying saucer!'

And she burst out sobbing.

Poor little Binkie! Pam and Barbara even felt sorry for Susie too. They quickly helped the two terrified girls into the shed, made them sit down, and gave them some lemonade. It was the end of a bottle left over from the Seven's last meeting.

'It's all a trick!' said Jack to the girls, crossly. 'They've got you to let them into the shed, and next moment they'll be laughing in your faces!'

'Ooh, this is *horrible*!' said Susie, feeling better now she had drunk the lemonade. 'I've never tasted anything so disgusting in my life! Honestly, people who *boast* of belonging to a Secret Society might at least –'

Then she suddenly stopped right in the middle of her sentence! What had she thought of? She looked at each of the Seven in turn, just as Binkie had done, and then she screamed. 'The flying saucer!' And she put her hands over her ears. 'Oh, that awful siren – and all the smoke! It's all coming back to me now!'

'Blue smoke!' said Binkie.

'No, it was red smoke!' Susie protested.

'No, it wasn't, it was blue, and then it turned green and *then* it turned red!'

14

'There you are!' said Susie. 'I *was* right!'

'Oh, just listen to them!' said Jack crossly. 'They've made up this story and learnt it off by heart – except they can't agree about the colour of the smoke!'

Colin suddenly thought of something – and started searching the little girls' pockets.

'What on earth are you doing?' George asked him.

'Just looking to see if they've got any onions,' said Colin grimly, and seeing his friend's surprised expression, he explained: 'To make them cry, of course!'

But Susie and Binkie didn't have any onions in their pockets. Colin even sniffed their hands, but he had to admit his idea was wrong. 'No, they aren't faking,' he said. 'Those are genuine tears!'

'Wait a minute!' said Jack, going up to the little girls. He wiped a tear off Susie's cheek with his finger-tip. 'No, it isn't glycerine!' he said, disappointed. 'I read a magazine article saying that film actors use glycerine to look like tears. The glycerine doesn't dry up like water would,' he explained.

'They don't believe us!' moaned Susie, flinging her arms round her friend's neck.

'And it's all true!' said Binkie. 'We didn't make up any of it – it's in all the newspapers!'

'Exactly!' said Jack. 'Only too easy for you little horrors to make up a story out of what's in the news!'

At these words the two girls burst out crying again. Janet had not said anything since they arrived. Now she stepped forward. 'Suppose they *are* telling the truth?' she asked. Her own voice trembled a little, but she turned to face the rest of the Seven bravely. 'I think you're all being very silly and stuck-up!' she said. 'I suppose you think nobody can have an adventure except *you*, and Susie and Binkie aren't good enough for anything exciting to happen to them! You feel as if they'd taken something that was yours by right, don't you?'

None of the rest of the Seven could think of anything to say. Janet might be the youngest of them – but at heart they knew she'd hit the nail on the head. They didn't like to think of those two little nuisances seeing something as exciting as a flying saucer. It ought to have been the Seven who saw it! After all, they prided themselves on seeing more than most people could. And now they'd been unlucky, and somebody else had seen a flying saucer instead of them!

There was a long and thoughtful silence. Scamper was puzzled. He had no idea what was going on, but he wanted to break the silence. He began prancing about, barking cheerfully – and the children began to talk again.

'Where did you see it?' asked Pam.

'Was it long ago?' enquired George.

Now they were all asking questions. Because thinking of what Janet had said, they realised that even if they hadn't seen a flying saucer yet – well, they had a good chance of seeing one in the near future, hadn't they?

## Chapter Two

## A STARTLING SIGHT

It was nearly dark. The children heard the church clock striking eight. They had all managed to get permission to go out after supper, just for once, since the weather was still so fine. For the last twenty minutes or so, they had been searching the hillside that led up to the ruins of Torling Castle.

Susie and Binkie were acting as their guides. Keeping close together and holding hands, the two little girls made their way timidly forward. Their teeth were chattering. Scamper went ahead, as if he thought that would help to reassure them. Nobody was talking much, though every now and then Peter would ask, 'Now what? This way or that way?'

And Susie and Binkie would nod or point to show which way the Seven ought to go.

As the children went on uphill it was getting darker all the time. Soon they came to a little plantation of fir trees, which had rather a gloomy look about them in the dusk. The moon was rising, casting pale light over the landscape and making shadows stand out more clearly.

'Ugh!' shivered Pam. 'This is getting creepy!'

As the children passed some bushes, they heard a rustling in the leaves. They all stopped dead, and Binkie let out a shriek!

Then, much to their alarm, the Seven and the two little girls heard a sinister creaking sound – and the next moment a huge owl with yellow eyes rose heavily into the air above the bushes.

'I'm not going a step further!' said Susie, pale with fright.

'I'm going home!' whispered Binkie. She was trembling all over.

'Now come on, you promised to guide us!' said Peter. 'You're not going to let us down now, just because of a perfectly harmless owl!'

'You can go on without us!' said Susie, who could be very obstinate.

'Anyway, you're nearly there,' said Binkie. She was biting her nails. 'See those three trees in the middle of the bushes over there? Well, that's – that's –'

But she was so scared that she couldn't finish her sentence.

'Is that where it was?' asked Peter eagerly.

Susie nodded.

'Come on!' said Jack firmly.

'What about *us*?' wailed the two little girls.

'I'll stay with you, if you like,' Pam offered generously.

'Yes, and Janet and Barbara can stay here too,' Peter decided. 'And George, if you don't mind *too* much –'

'That's all right,' said George. 'I'll look after the

girls!' He was quite good-natured about it, although he would rather *not* have been left behind. He hadn't been very well during the winter, and the doctor had said he thought it might be asthma and George had better not take too much violent exercise for the time being. It was annoying, but he hoped he'd soon be better. And he realised he still felt rather weaker than usual, so that if a flying saucer happened to land or take off right in front of him, he wouldn't be able to run for it as fast as his friends! All things considered, it was more sensible for him to stay with the girls and make sure they were all right if anything alarming happened.

'Do be careful!' Janet begged the three other boys in a whisper as they set off into the dark.

'It's all right. We've got good old Scamper with us!' Colin told her. He hoped he sounded braver than he felt, but his voice gave him away!

Peter and Scamper led the way, with Jack and Colin after them. They all kept their eyes firmly fixed on the group of trees that Binkie had pointed out. Three trees in the middle of a thicket of bushes! That was the place.

When they were quite close, the three boys got down flat on the ground like Red Indians, and Scamper lay down as well, with his nose between his paws.

They waited in silence for several minutes, peering round them. There was nothing moving anywhere, except for the leaves rustling in the gentle wind.

'Come on!' Peter whispered.

He began making his way towards the three trees. Jack and Colin followed him. Scamper didn't make a sound as he leaped along beside them.

They soon reached the bushes, and stopped at the foot of the group of three trees. Somehow they didn't like the idea of making a noise which might give away the fact that they were there, so they made signs to each other instead. Colin pointed to the inside of the thicket of bushes, then put his thumb in the air to show that he couldn't see anything wrong in *there*. Peter swept his arm round, as if to say that everything around them seemed all right too. Jack jerked his head towards the trees, suggesting that it might be a good idea to go closer.

The three boys went on, wriggling through the long grass like eels. Scamper seemed to realise that there might be danger, and he was panting as quietly as he could.

Peter was still leading the way, taking all possible precautions so as not to make any noise. Very, very carefully he pushed the grass down in front of him, and he made sure that there weren't any twigs that he might crack in his way. He was so excited that he was perspiring – and he was ready to take off as fast as a hare any moment, if danger *should* threaten. Colin and Jack were crawling along in his wake.

Only a very little way to go now, and they would be at the exact spot where Susie and Binkie had said they saw the flying saucer land!

Peter was tense all over. One last effort! All his muscles contracted, he took his weight on his elbows, and hauled himself the last little bit further.

And now, at last, he could see!

Or rather, he *couldn't* see, because there wasn't anything to be seen! Nothing but what you might expect to see in the ordinary way – just the grass on the other side of the three trees.

'It's taken off again!' he shouted, jumping to his feet.

His two friends joined him at once.

'Not a trace of it!' Colin agreed. He was examining the ground.

'No, because that flying saucer never existed!' said Jack, furiously. 'Those two little nuisances have tricked us again. Oh, just *wait* till I get my hands on Susie!'

'Scamper, you go and find them!' Peter told the spaniel. 'Fetch! Susie and Binkie – fetch! And the others too. Off you go – good dog!'

Scamper took off like lightning. They could hear him barking as he shot away into the darkness.

Then Colin remembered that he had a torch with him. He got it out of his pocket and switched it on. Now the girls and George wouldn't have any difficulty in finding their way – the beam of the torch would guide them.

Sure enough, George, Pam, Janet and Barbara arrived less than a minute later, along with Susie and Binkie.

'They were only telling a story!' Jack told George and the girls. 'All fibs! I'll tell you what, we'll leave them here on their own all night, just to punish them!'

'No! No!' cried Susie. She was terrified.

'We did see a flying saucer, we *did*!' wailed Binkie, her eyes filling with tears again.

'Prove it!' said Peter, bluntly.

'Yes, and how are you going to explain the fact that it didn't leave any marks on the ground?' asked

Colin, grabbing Susie's pigtails.

'I don't know anything about it — I don't *understand*!' wept poor Susie, sobbing.

'You're a couple of fine little liars, aren't you?' said Barbara, sarcastically. 'Now let me tell you —'

WHEEEEEEEE!

A shrill whistling sound suddenly pierced the darkness — and all of a sudden the hillside was glowing with reddish light.

'The saucer!' shrieked Pam, pointing at the sky.

She stood there with her mouth open, rooted to the spot with fright. Her friends were petrified too! Their eyes were popping as they gazed at this incredible sight.

A disc of bright light, less than fifty metres away and as dazzling as the sun, was slowly coming down to earth. It was surrounded by a sort of halo of red smoke.

Scamper, who couldn't make out what on earth was going on, was running round and round in circles — but the others all stood perfectly still.

The Seven saw the flying saucer stop, quite suddenly, while it was still ten metres or so above the ground. Then they saw an amazing phenomenon. That smoky halo was changing colour!

It turned purple instead of red, then violet, and then turquoise blue. And then the saucer started coming down again, slowly and smoothly, and settled gently on the ground. At that moment a light started going round and round on top of it, sweeping its beam

around the landscape.

When the bright light passed over the children, Susie and Binkie flung themselves to the ground, screaming.

And then, just as if it had heard the scream, the flying saucer took off again! It rose slowly from the ground, and the whistle became louder than ever. Peter and the others had to put their hands over their ears.

Once the flying saucer was about a hundred metres up it began moving sideways, parallel with the ground and very fast. In less than five seconds it had disappeared.

Everything around the children was dark and silent again.

It was several minutes before the Seven could move at all. They were staring up at the sky. Susie and Binkie were lying in the grass at their feet, keeping perfectly still too.

Scamper was the one who brought them all back to

life. He ran from one of the children to another, licking a hand here and a knee there. He jumped up, begged, barked, did all he could to get the children moving again. He didn't like it when they stood so still – it just wasn't normal!

Peter was the first to recover the use of his tongue. 'Let's go home,' he said in an expressionless sort of voice.

'It might be dangerous,' suggested Jack.

Pam came back to life again too, and went over to Susie and Binkie. 'Come on, do get up!' she said. 'You can't just stay there!'

She and Barbara helped Susie up, while George and Colin got Binkie back on her feet.

Peter looked at Janet. She was doing her best to be brave, but he could see she was still so terrified she could hardly move. He went over to her and gave her a quick hug.

'I want Mummy!' said Janet, trying not to cry. 'I want Mummy!'

Peter assured her that they'd be back at home in Old Mill House in less than half an hour's time – and then he gave the word for them all to start back to the village.

It was hard for the Seven to get to sleep that night. They couldn't stop thinking of the astonishing things they'd seen. And then, at midnight, there was a violent storm. Thunder growled and lightning flashed for over two hours, making it harder than ever for them to sleep peacefully. What an extra-ordinary day – no wonder if they had strange dreams! But would they ever find out any more about that flying saucer?

## Chapter Three

## TEMPORARY MEMBERS OF THE SEVEN

The Secret Seven held a meeting early next afternoon, in the shed in Peter and Janet's garden.

'U.F.O.,' whispered Pam as she tapped on the door, giving their new password.

Peter opened the door. 'Late again!' he said, as he shut it behind her.

'Well, *someone* has to arrive last!' snapped Pam, feeling cross with both Peter and herself.

She sat down with the others, in between Barbara and Janet. The boys were sitting on old orange boxes opposite the girls. Scamper looked as if he thought he was chairing the meeting, stretched out full length on the floor in the very middle of the shed.

'Now, let's begin!' said Peter, once Pam was sitting down. 'I've been thinking hard about what we ought to do next.'

He stopped and looked round at everyone, very seriously.

'We won't tell anyone else what we saw!' he said firmly. 'So don't go talking about it, or dropping any hints. It's all top secret, understand? We're keeping this adventure to ourselves!'

'Right!' said George.

'Right!' everyone else echoed him.

'But what about Susie and Binkie?' asked Jack. 'You've forgotten about *them*!'

'No, I haven't,' Peter contradicted him. 'And they certainly *are* a problem. They saw the whole thing too.'

'And come to think of it, it's thanks to them *we* saw anything at all,' Pam pointed out.

Janet shuddered slightly. She still wasn't sure that she liked this adventure. It might have been nicer *not* to see anything!

'But we can't let them keep going round with us!' said Colin, horrified. 'They'll be such an awful nuisance the whole time – you know what they're like!'

'Yes, but if we leave them out they'll give everything away the very first chance they get,' Barbara told him. 'Just as you said – we all know what they're like!'

'Yes, I agree,' said Peter. 'The moment we tell them to go away and forget about it, they'll go away all right – but they'll tell the entire village!'

'Well, what do *you* suggest, Peter?' Janet asked her brother.

'They'll have to share in this adventure. There's nothing else we can do!'

'Peter, you're never going to let Susie and Binkie join the Secret Seven, are you?' cried Colin, horrified. The two little girls had been pestering the Seven to let them join for ages, and however often Peter explained that they just couldn't, and anyway then it wouldn't *be* a Secret Seven Society any more, they never would give up!

'If you let *them* join, I'm leaving!' said Jack, furiously. 'You can jolly well have Susie *instead* of me!'

'Calm down, for goodness' sake!' said Peter.

'But Peter, we really *can't* let them join. It's against the rules of the Society!' said George.

'All right then, if you've got a better idea, let's hear it!' shouted Peter, just managing to make himself heard above all the indignant noise.

Everyone fell silent. No one could think of anything to say. Scamper was feeling rather worried – he looked round at all the children with his big, black eyes opened very wide.

'What *I* suggest is, we let them be temporary members, just for this adventure. And we make it perfectly clear that they can't join in anything else the Secret Seven do,' said Pam, after a few moments.

'That's what I was going to say too,' Barbara backed her up. 'It's the best solution.'

'I warn you,' said Jack, gloomily, 'any trouble out of those two little pests, and I'm resigning from the Society!'

'All right, you've said that already!' Peter told him a little impatiently. 'Anyone else against the idea of temporary membership?'

He waited a few moments, but nobody spoke up.

'Right,' said Peter. 'Motion carried! Binkie and Susie can join in the rest of this adventure with us – but they're not going to be part of the Seven after that. Now, would one of you like to go and tell them?'

'I'll go,' Janet offered, getting up.

But she didn't have to go far! When she opened the door of the shed, what did she see but those two annoying little girls themselves, standing just outside!

'They've been listening!' shouted Jack. 'Of all the cheek! We *can't* have them in an adventure – it'd be sheer disaster!'

'Oh yes?' said Susie. She seemed to have got over her fright of the day before, and was as maddening as ever! 'If it hadn't been for us you'd be having very boring holidays!'

'You've *got* to have us in your silly old Society

now!' said Binkie triumphantly. 'Otherwise we'll go and tell everyone about the flying saucer!'

'All right, all right, come in!' said Peter, rather reluctantly.

The two little girls promptly came into the shed. They looked all round it proudly, exploring every corner, as if it belonged to them.

'Not a bad place you've got here!' said Susie in a teasing voice, sitting down carefully on an orange box.

'Yes — we couldn't really appreciate it yesterday!' said Binkie, in the same annoying way. 'Look at all the nice furnishings! Ooh, what good taste!' She sounded as if she were imitating something she'd heard a grown-up say.

'You do the housework yourselves, do you?' asked Susie, letting her eyes stray to a large cobweb in the corner of an old shelf.

'Make them shut up or I'll jolly well *strangle* them!' said Jack, quite pale with rage.

'You're always saying that!' said Susie, roaring with laughter.

'Well, this time I'll *do* it!' Jack yelled. He leaped on his sister like a tiger, knocking over the orange box in his haste. Susie tumbled off and fell on her back, and Jack flung himself at her. He was so cross he actually *was* starting to twist her pigtails round her neck.

'Here, stop it, Jack!' shouted Peter. 'That's quite enough of that!'

Scamper agreed, barking loudly.

George and Colin dragged Jack off his sister, and Susie sat up, trembling. This time, she knew she'd gone too far – and Jack had really frightened her.

Jack turned his back on his sister, and drank a large glass of lemonade to calm himself down.

'If we're going to spend all our time quarrelling, this adventure won't get very far!' said Peter. 'Susie and Binkie, if you've just come here to make trouble then you can forget about being temporary members of the Secret Seven and go home again!'

'Anything you say!' Binkie giggled. 'But you know we'll tell everyone about it, the moment you throw us out!'

'Tell everyone about what?' asked Colin, suddenly seeing the Seven's advantage. 'Tell them you saw a flying saucer while you were out with us?'

'That's right!' said Susie.

'Well then, *we'll* just say you're telling lies!' replied Colin. 'And people know what a lot of fibs you two girls tell – so they're much more likely to believe us than you, aren't they? Not to mention the fact that it'll be seven of us against two of you!'

Susie and Binkie hadn't thought of that! They sat down again without a word, defeated.

'Don't bother to sit down!' Peter told them. 'Not if you want to come with us, that is! Because we're going straight back to that hill that leads up to Torling Castle – now!'

## Chapter Four

## SAUCER-HUNTING BY DAYLIGHT

Half an hour later, the Seven were climbing the hill that led towards the ruins of Torling Castle again. The two little nuisances were with them, of course! Susie and Binkie weren't nearly so scared exploring the place by daylight, and Peter had very kindly let them have Scamper with them, so that they'd be sure to feel perfectly safe.

The children hurried to the place where they had seen the flying saucer the night before. They reached the fir trees, and the place where Susie and Binkie had stopped and refused to go on, and then they easily found the group of three trees towards which Peter, Jack and Colin had crawled so carefully.

'Here we are,' said Peter, putting out his arm to make everyone stop.

'The flying saucer appeared on our left,' Colin remembered, pointing. 'And it came down to earth near those large bushes.'

'Are you sure?' asked Barbara. 'I thought it was closer than that.'

'So did I,' agreed George.

'No, I don't think so,' Jack said. 'I remember seeing the bushes move when it took off again.'

'That doesn't prove anything,' said Binkie – as if *she* knew anything about it.

'Well, we'd better go and investigate close to,' said Peter, interrupting this argument. 'It may have left some marks on the ground.'

They went over to the spot where they thought it had landed, and Peter told them to spread out and go very slowly, examining every bit of the ground as they passed over it.

'Grass, grass and more grass, that's all!' said Susie impatiently, after a minute or two.

'You can't expect results straightaway!' her brother pointed out. 'Anyone can see *you're* not used to adventures and mysteries! It takes patience and thoroughness to solve a mystery – if you know what patience and thoroughness mean!'

'You're just being horrible!' his sister snapped back. 'Who do you think you are?'

'Stop that!' said Peter.

'He began it this time,' Susie said, defending herself.

'Yes, he did,' Peter admitted. He turned towards Jack, raising his voice, and said, 'If you two don't stop quarrelling this minute, I'm not letting *either* of you be in the adventure! Understand?'

Jack didn't say anything. He was feeling very cross – and cross with himself too. Susie felt very pleased with herself, however! She was delighted to have got her big brother into trouble with the leader of the Seven.

The children went on searching for any traces of the flying saucer, some on their knees, others crawling about on all fours. Janet went methodically from one tuft of grass to another. After several minutes of this, however, they realised that the U.F.O. couldn't have left any marks at all.

Then, suddenly, George uttered an exclamation.

At first all the others thought he must have found something really important – but it was only a rabbit hole!

'I saw the rabbit's little head looking out!' said George, who liked animals. 'It was brown, with white ears. Poor little thing – it thought I was hunting it!'

Peter couldn't help smiling. 'Are you quite sure it wasn't an extra-terrestrial rabbit?' he asked jokingly.

'I'm afraid I didn't have time to ask it,' said George, in the same sort of voice.

'And what do you kids think you're up to here?' somebody suddenly said in a deep, angry voice behind the boys.

Peter turned round at once – and stood rooted to the spot with surprise.

Five men had come up, without making the slightest noise. Now they were standing quite close to the children. They were tall, dressed in brown dungarees, and they looked very threatening.

'You've got no business around here,' said the biggest of the men. 'Go on, clear out – fast!'

Scamper bared his teeth. He didn't like the way this man talked one bit.

'What's the matter with our looking for mushrooms, then?' asked Colin defiantly.

'What, without so much as a basket to put them in?' asked one of the men in a sarcastic voice. 'Think you can pull the wool over our eyes that easily, young man?'

'Go on, be off with you!' one of his friends

threatened the children. 'Or I'll see you all get a good hiding!'

'I'd like to see you try it!' said Susie bravely, if rather cheekily, and she took a step forward. Scamper kept beside her, barking.

'I'll soon shut *you* up, little girl!' said the biggest man angrily, lunging towards the children.

'Here, Susie, come on!' Jack whispered, taking his sister's hand. 'I know how you feel, but you'll just make things worse!'

Peter, too, had decided that it would be sensible to beat a retreat.

'Fine!' he said. 'Have the place all to yourselves! It's full of death-cap mushrooms up here, you know! Indistinguishable from the real edible mushroom. I expect a nice fry-up of death-cap mushrooms for breakfast will do you no end of good!'

And with this parting shot, he took to his heels and ran, followed by his friends. Brave Scamper stayed behind a moment or so longer, to make sure they got safely away.

The biggest of the men moved towards the good dog to chase him off, but when he saw Scamper's bared teeth he thought it might be better to wait for the spaniel to go and rejoin the children of his own accord – and that was just what Scamper eventually did.

'Oh, thank goodness, there you are!' said Janet lovingly when she saw him come bounding up. '*Good* dog! You were a great help, just as usual!'

The Seven and Susie and Binkie had not gone very far. They had taken refuge in a little wood of pine trees.

'What a nerve! Did you ever know anything like it?' said Colin. He was furious.

'Who *are* those men? And what are they up to?' asked Barbara, puzzled.

'I've never seen them in the village, I'm sure,' said Peter. 'And it looks as if we were in their way!'

'How could we have been in their way, just searching the grass?' asked Jack.

'Well, they could have been looking for the same thing we were,' said Peter.

'Do you mean the flying saucer?' asked the bewildered Pam.

'Or traces of it.'

'But – but that would mean they saw it yesterday evening too! And they were somewhere near us in the dark!' Janet said, suddenly realising how close they might have been. It wasn't a very nice idea.

'I'm going back to the village!' said Binkie, with a shudder.

'That's not a bad notion,' Susie agreed, though she herself was quick to recover from the fright they'd had. '*You* may think this is a fascinating adventure for your silly old Secret Seven, but *I* call it just plain dangerous! Over the last twenty-four hours I've nearly been eaten by an owl and then kidnapped and taken away in a flying saucer, and now we've got five horrible men with knives after us!'

'Knives? *I* didn't see any knives,' said Jack in surprise. 'What makes you think they've got knives?'

'They *do* have knives! Didn't you see their faces?' said Susie.

Jack looked more baffled than ever.

'Anybody with a face like that is *sure* to be carrying a knife,' Binkie explained. *She* could follow Susie's rather peculiar reasoning perfectly well!

'Oh, all right,' said Peter. He didn't want any more quarrelling among themselves just now. 'But you girls needn't be frightened any more. We're safe here in these trees.'

'Woof! Woof! Woof!' Three barks were heard in the undergrowth.

'Something's happened to Scamper!' cried Janet, very worried.

'Where is he?' asked Pam, looking round for the spaniel.

'He was here a moment ago!' said George, taking a good look himself.

'I hope to goodness he's not gone back to attack those horrible men or anything,' said Colin, anxiously.

'Scamper!' Peter called the dog. 'Scamper! Here, boy! Scamper – where *are* you?'

But the little spinney of trees seemed to muffle his shouts. At any rate, there wasn't any answer.

The Seven were imagining awful things. Suppose Scamper had gone back and barked at the men, and one of them had hit him? He might be hurt, or even lying on the grass unconscious!

'Oh, what a *beastly* day!' said Janet, rather tearfully. 'I think we'd better give up this saucer-hunt!'

But just then they all heard Scamper's joyful barking nearby.

'Here he is!' cried Jack. 'On his way back to us, safe and sound!'

'But what on earth is he carrying?' said Barbara in surprise. She had seen that the dog had something in his mouth.

'Good gracious!' said Peter. 'A bar of chocolate!'

Proudly, Scamper laid his find at his young master's feet.

'*Futura Chocolate*,' Colin read out loud. 'Look – that's what it says on the wrapper, in gold letters.'

He passed the bar of chocolate to his friends, and they all looked at it.

'I don't think I've ever had any Futura chocolate,' said Pam.

'I've never even *heard* of that brand,' said George.

'Scamper, who gave it to you?' Peter asked.

But all the dog said, naturally, was, 'Woof! Woof!'

'I hope it wasn't those men we met just now,' said Janet.

'Woof! Woof!' Scamper repeated. Then he set off at a run, stopped, barked twice again, and turned round to look at the children.

'He wants us to follow him,' said Jack. 'Come on, everyone!'

And all together, the Seven, Susie and Binkie set off after the dog.

'That's right, Scamper – good boy! Show us where

43

you found this chocolate,' Peter told him.

Scamper seemed very pleased that they had understood. He led the children on after him, wagging his plumy golden tail. He went right through the wood, along by the side of it for a little way, and then turned off over the hillside. After a few moments, he stopped beside a thick clump of bramble bushes.

'Woof! Woof!'

'He's trying to tell us he found the chocolate here, right inside all those brambles,' said Janet.

'Yes – look, you can still see the way he went,' Colin noticed. Sure enough, Scamper had made a little tunnel going in among the thorny brambles.

'I'm going in,' said Peter.

'Me too!' said Jack, following Peter's lead.

The two boys plunged straight into the brambles through the narrow passage Scamper had made for them. It hurt more than they'd expected! There were yells of, 'Ouch! These brambles are prickly! Oh, my poor fingers!'

'Can you see anything?' George asked them, peering into the bramble bushes.

'Yes, thorns! *Ow!*' said Jack.

'However did a bar of chocolate land in a place like that?' Susie asked. She wasn't as sure as the Seven that Scamper knew what he was doing!

'Fell from the sky, I expect,' said Binkie, laughing.

But she didn't know how right she was! At that very moment, Peter let out an exclamation.

'The flying saucer!' he cried.

*Chapter Five*

## AN UNEXPECTED FIND

'What?' said the children, standing outside the clump of brambles.

'The flying saucer!' Jack repeated. 'And it's full of chocolate!'

'What on earth are you going on about?' said Colin. He couldn't make head or tail of this!

'Just as Jack says – we've found the flying saucer and it's full of chocolate!' Peter said, roaring with laughter.

'They're laughing at *us*!' said George indignantly.

'Well, if that's what you two in there are doing, I'm coming in for a look myself, and never mind the thorns!' said Colin, plunging through the brambles. And George followed him. That left just the five bewildered girls standing outside the clump of bramble bushes.

When George and Colin got into the middle of the bushes, and joined Peter and Jack, they stopped in surprise. Every word their friends had said was true! The flying saucer had come down at an awkward angle in the middle of the thorny brambles, and as it landed it had opened, spilling out a cargo of chocolate.

'Why, it's no bigger than a tractor wheel after all!' said George, disappointed.

'So it isn't a *real* flying saucer!' Colin said. He was rather annoyed to find that the adventure was turning out to be more comical than exciting.

'FUTURA – THE CHOCOLATE OF TOMORROW!' Peter read out loud, pointing to the gold lettering painted on the flying saucer.

'It's an advertisement, I bet!' said Jack. 'Look, there are at least fifty chocolate bars inside the thing!'

He put his hand into the saucer and brought the bars out, counting them as he did so. 'Forty-five!' he said, bringing out the last. 'Well, I was very nearly right. Hang on a minute – there's a piece of paper at the very bottom there.'

And he picked up a sort of little poster with a gold border and a red seal on it.

Peter read what it said out loud. The words were printed in curly lettering.

'The finder of this FUTURA saucer has won a top prize in the great FUTURA game. Signed: Andrew Latimer, Chairman and Managing Director, Futura Chocolate, Castleford.'

Colin took the piece of paper from Peter, to see what it said for himself.

'Just a silly competition!' he said grumpily. 'A sort of publicity stunt! And like idiots we went and fell for it!'

'We weren't the only ones,' George pointed out. 'All the newspapers were going on about flying saucers. It was even on television!'

'Yes, I suppose it was quite a *clever* publicity stunt,' Jack agreed. 'Soon everybody will know about Futura, the chocolate of tomorrow. You've got to admit the flying saucer was a good notion!'

Suddenly Barbara's voice brought them back to earth.

'Whatever *are* you boys doing in there?' she asked. 'Come on out, with whatever you've found. We want a look at it too!'

'All right – coming!' Peter said.

The four boys made their way along the tunnel through the bramble bushes again, passing out the chocolate they had found. Susie and Binkie couldn't get over it! 'And another!' they kept saying, as bar followed bar. '*And* another! And *another*!'

Night was falling when the children got home to the village, with their pockets full of chocolate. Susie and Binkie had been eating rather a lot of it, taking no notice of Pam and Janet, who warned them they'd get a stomach-ache. They just went on eating! They were on their third bar now.

The other children were more sensible. They'd only had a few little pieces of chocolate each. Scamper had been given some too. Now he was having a game with the frogs who lived in the ditch by the roadside, jumping at the poor things to scare them!

When the village came in sight, the children heard a car coming along the road behind them. They quickly got into single file, for there was no pavement along this narrow country lane. And the car was certainly driving very fast, right in the middle of the road. It roared noisily past the children, and they noticed that it hadn't got its lights on, although it was nearly dark now.

'I say, did you see that?' said Barbara, in surprise. 'Those were the five men who chased us away from the hillside – I'm sure they were! There were five people in that car, and they were about the right size!'

The other children thought Barbara was right. What had those five men been doing since they all met? And where were they going to now? And who exactly were they? The Seven couldn't help wondering – but they had no answers to any of their questions! The flying saucer might have turned out to be all a hoax – however, they still couldn't explain the peculiar way those men had behaved.

After supper, Peter and Janet were watching television with their parents. The news programme contained another item about flying saucers. Peter couldn't help winking at his sister.

'Ridiculous story!' said Peter's father, puffing at his pipe. He blew three smoke-rings.

'Do you know, the lady in the Post Office told me that someone told *her* he'd actually seen one of these saucers in the sky, somewhere over towards Torling Castle last night,' said Peter's mother.

Peter and Janet simply dared not look at each other, for fear of bursting out laughing.

'Some people are crazy!' said their father. 'You get one person with a wild imagination talking nonsense of that kind – and it immediately affects lots of other over-excited folk who all claim to have seen the same phenomenon!'

The newsreader went on to say that over the last

twenty-four hours, sightings of flying saucers had been reported all over the country.

Peter frowned when he heard this. How could he and the rest of the Seven have seen the flying saucer, when other people hundreds of kilometres away were supposed to have spotted it too?

Did they mean the same saucer? The one belonging to Futura Chocolate? Peter doubted that. *His* flying saucer, the one he'd discovered among the brambles, was only an advertising stunt. It couldn't possibly have covered such distances within a few minutes!

So there must be several flying saucers. Did they all belong to Futura Chocolate?

Peter felt a little shiver run down his spine. He had just realised that, after all, Futura Chocolate could be taking advantage of a *genuine* invasion from outer space to promote its publicity campaign. If so, things were rather serious, and for all he knew he might be about to see a little green man coming in through his bedroom window, which was not a nice idea at all!

When he looked at Janet, he could see that the same nasty thought must have occurred to her. Her face was very pale, and her lips were trembling.

The children had all promised each other not to say anything about the flying saucer to any grown-ups — but Peter suddenly decided that it would be better to tell his parents after all. He took the piece of paper about the chocolate and the prize out of his pocket, and showed it to his father.

His father read it twice, connected what it said with the news report on television, and what Peter's mother had said about the lady in the Post Office, and then he burst out laughing.

'So you children found it!' he said, laughing so hard he seemed as if he might swallow his pipe! 'Well, congratulations! Ha, ha, ha! You were cleverer than any of those other idiots who believed in the U.F.O. stories! Ho, ho, ho!'

Peter's mother took the piece of paper in her turn and read what it said. 'Well, what a ridiculous story!' she exclaimed. 'I call it quite mad!' And she too began laughing at the hoax Futura Chocolate had pulled off.

Peter and Janet weren't laughing, though. They were sitting there thinking hard. They just didn't know *what* to think of the flying saucers any more.

## Chapter Six

## A VISIT TO CASTLEFORD

Next day Peter and Janet's father made sure that work on the farm was going all right, and told all his men what to do, so that he could take some time off. He had said he would take Peter and Janet and their friends into Castleford to collect their prize from the Futura Chocolate firm.

Peter, Janet and Scamper came hurrying up as he was starting his van.

'My word, you two look smart!' he said, letting them into the back. Peter was wearing grey trousers, a white shirt and a blue blazer, and Janet had changed out of the jeans she liked to wear in the holidays and was dressed in a pleated pink skirt and a matching blouse.

'Mother's idea!' Peter explained, as he shut the van door after them. 'She thought we ought to be dressed in our best if we were going to claim the prize! I wasn't all that keen on the idea myself!'

'Never mind,' said Janet. 'Scamper got away without having any ribbons tied round his head, didn't you, Scamper, old boy?'

Their father smiled as he put the van into gear and drove it out of the garage.

'Well, shall we stop at George's first?' he asked.

'Yes, let's,' said Peter. 'He lives closest.'

So they picked up George first, and then Barbara, Pam and Colin. Last of all was Jack, who lived furthest from Old Mill House, but he had come part of the way to meet the van, and the others saw him coming along the road before they reached his house. Peter's father put the brakes on, and in a moment Jack was in the van with the other members of the Secret Seven.

'Susie's not coming!' he told them at once. 'She's got an awful stomach-ache. She wasn't very well in the night, and she's staying in bed this morning.'

'What about Binkie?' asked Pam.

'Same thing with Binkie!' said Jack, with a broad grin. 'Her mother telephoned us to say she wasn't coming either – she's in bed too!'

'Well, it just serves them right!' Colin said. 'We did warn them. I'm not a bit sorry for those two little pests!'

The van was out of the village now, and driving along the road to Castleford, a big town about an hour's drive away. As it passed Torling Castle, standing up on the hillside, the Seven couldn't help glancing up at the spot where they had found the flying saucer, and then further uphill to where the five men had been searching. But there was no sign of anything moving there today.

Peter wondered if this might be the end of the flying saucer after all. Being an honest boy, he realised that perhaps he'd rather *enjoyed* scaring himself with ideas about real U.F.O.s after that television news item last night.

It was a fine day, his friends were happy and cheerful, and they were off to collect a prize! So why try to cast a gloomy shadow over everything?

Peter took a deep breath, wound down the van window next to his seat and let the wind blow in on his face. It was lovely mild weather – spring was really here! What was there to worry about?

At eleven o'clock the van passed the sign saying that the town of Castleford began here, and Peter's father stopped near a road junction to ask a woman who was out shopping the way to the chocolate firm's factory and offices.

'Excuse me, can you tell us where to find Futura Chocolate?' he asked through his open window.

'Futura Chocolate, did you say?' the woman asked in surprise. 'Sorry, I've never heard of it. Are you sure you've got the name right?'

'Yes, quite sure,' said Peter's father. 'Well, never mind – thanks all the same! We're sure to find the place in the end.'

He drove on, and stopped again at a crossing where a policeman was directing the traffic.

'Can you tell us where to find the Futura Chocolate building, please?'

'Futura Chocolate, sir?' said the policeman,

thinking. 'Can't say I've ever heard *that* name! A new firm, would it be?'

'Well, I suppose that's possible,' said Peter's father, who obviously wasn't sure.

'There's the Black Cat chocolate factory – but they were talking of closing that down,' said the policeman. 'Can't think of anything else, I'm afraid. Futura – no, sorry, I can't help you.'

Peter's father thanked him and drove on again.

'How funny,' said Peter. 'You'd think people would *notice* a chocolate factory, wouldn't you? I mean, it must be quite a big place!'

'I've thought of a new advertising slogan for them!' said Colin. '*Futura, the elusive phantom chocolate*! What do you think of that?'

'It's not bad,' said Barbara, 'but it doesn't help us find the actual place where we want to go!'

'I think we'll go to the Black Cat building,' said Peter's father. 'If it's another chocolate factory, they must know there where we can find the rival firm!'

They had no difficulty at all in finding the Black Cat works. Everybody in Castleford knew where *they* were, and a lot of people had either worked there or knew somebody who had.

'First turn left, and then it's the second street on the right,' said Janet, who had got the directions from a passing postman.

Her father turned left, and then second right, and a moment later the van drew up beside a factory fence.

'Hallo!' said Pam, as she got out of the van. 'Look,

they're just repainting that big sign outside the gate!'
    'F – U – T –' Jack read out aloud.

'FUTURA!' cried Colin. 'Well, that explains it! Futura Chocolate has taken the factory over from the Black Cat people!'

'Come on, let's hurry!' said Barbara impatiently. 'We'll soon find out all about it!'

Peter and Janet's father led the way into the building, and the Seven followed him. A pointer saying 'Visitors' showed them the way to a reception area. Scamper thought this was all very interesting! He was jumping about in a very lively way, panting hard, letting his tongue hang out, and rolling his eyes.

'Greedy thing – he can smell the chocolate!' Janet explained. She held tightly to his lead.

'Well, you can't blame him; it *does* smell good,' said

George. He helped her to keep the spaniel under control.

He was right. The closer they came to the reception area, the stronger the smell of chocolate grew. It was delicious! By the time they stopped at the reception desk, the air was full of it.

'We'd like to see Mr Latimer, please,' Peter's father told the girl at the desk.

'Have you got an appointment?' she asked.

'No, but here's our passport, so to speak,' Peter's father told her, and he showed her the piece of paper with the gold border.

'Oh, well done!' cried the girl. 'You're the first! Do come with me – Mr Latimer will be delighted to see you.'

They followed her along several corridors, and a little later they came to a kind of glass-walled over-pass from which you could look down into the works of the factory itself. The Seven were fascinated. What a sight – huge vats of steaming chocolate, with great blades stirring the mixture round and round! A little further on they saw assembly lines where the chocolate was being poured into moulds to cool, and then packed and labelled.

At last they came to the managing director's office. The receptionist knocked on the door, went in, and closed the door again behind her. The Seven could hear her inside the office explaining why they had come. Then she came out again and asked them to go in.

'Congratulations, children! Good work!' said Mr Latimer, coming to meet them. 'Do sit down, please!'

The receptionist brought some more chairs in, and soon they were all comfortably seated.

'I expect you've got a lot of questions you'd like to ask,' Mr Latimer suggested, smiling. 'And I'm here to answer them, so go ahead!'

Pam asked the first question. 'Please, Mr Latimer, can you explain why nobody ever seems to have heard of your Futura Chocolate?' she said. 'And why has it taken the place of the Black Cat chocolate factory?'

'Oh, that's soon answered!' said Mr Latimer, adjusting his glasses. 'Nobody's heard of Futura Chocolate because we've only just started making it. Even the good folk of Castleford don't know about it. We wanted to keep it a secret, you see, so as to make as big a publicity splash as possible.'

'What about the people working in the factory itself?' said Colin.

'We made them promise not to give the secret away. As I'm sure you can imagine, they've had a lot of fun over the last day or so, seeing what reactions we got to the advertising campaign.'

'What about the Black Cat factory?' asked Janet. 'Where does *that* come into the story?'

'The Black Cat was on the point of going out of business,' Mr Latimer explained. 'The firm hadn't been very well run. So my own firm bought it, and we're continuing to make chocolate here under the new brand name of Futura. The change-over went very smoothly indeed. All the right machinery, as you'll have seen on your way to this office, was already installed.'

'Tell us about the flying saucer,' asked Barbara.

'Yes, indeed!' said Mr Latimer. 'A much more interesting subject!'

'How does it work?' 'How's it driven?' 'Is it radar-controlled?' 'What made the smoke?' 'Can you follow its movements from this distance?' asked the children all at once.

'Phew! That certainly *is* a lot to answer all in one breath!' said Mr Latimer, smiling. 'However, I'll do my best! First, the saucer was an extremely light-weight model, made of a special new kind of plastic, and it worked on a form of automatic pilot. Once we had launched it on its way, we lost all contact with it.'

'Might that not have been dangerous?' asked Peter's father, who was finding all this very interesting.

'No, not in the least,' said Mr Latimer firmly. 'Being so light, and travelling at a maximum speed of thirty kilometres per hour, there wasn't any risk of its damaging anything in a collision. Also, it had a photo-electrical cell system able to detect any moving object or creature within twenty metres of itself.'

'But suppose it had come down on a roof – or crashed into the window of a house, or a shop's big plate-glass display window?' asked Jack.

'No danger of that either,' Mr Latimer told him.

'The saucer was flying only in an area well away from all busy roads or towns and villages. Its flight plan was worked out by highly qualified engineers, and was repeated once every half an hour. Look, here you are – here's a copy!'

He read out aloud what it said on the piece of paper he was showing his visitors.

'Cyclic system programme for Futura Flying Saucer.
1. Lateral movement left, speed thirty k.p.h.
2. Descent to ground. Smoke bombs set off. Sounding of siren.

3. Saucer hovers ten metres above ground. Second set of smoke bombs go off, with change of colours.
4. Landing. Gyroscopic light comes on. Duration of landing period, forty-five seconds.
5. Take-off. All lights switched on, smoke bomb still going off. Gyroscopic light switched off.
6. Ascent to height of one hundred metres. Smoke bombs extinguished. Siren stops sounding.
7. Lateral movement right, speed thirty k.p.h.'

The children listened spellbound.

'And that programme is repeated twice an hour over an area of ten square kilometres,' Mr Latimer explained. 'After three hours' activity, the saucer comes down again and remains on the ground for another two hours. That's the minimum necessary period for it to recharge its batteries. The saucer will function for only a hundred hours on automatic pilot – call it four days. Then it stops for good.'

'That's simply amazing!' breathed Colin, looking at the sheet of paper that Mr Latimer had handed the children.

'I ought to have said,' Mr Latimer added, 'that of course we had permission from the local authorities to carry out this advertising campaign.'

'Of course!' exclaimed George. 'Now we know why the police and the Army seemed to be taking no interest in the flying saucers – it did seem surprising!'

'I suppose all the news reporters were in the know too?' said Barbara.

'Oh no, *they* didn't know anything about it,' said Mr Latimer. 'We thought it was safe to bet they'd give us as much publicity as we could wish for – and we turned out to be right!'

'You *were*!' agreed Jack. 'One hundred per cent right.'

What an amazing story! But there was one thing about it all which Peter still couldn't explain to himself – and he was wondering if the Seven's latest adventure had really come to an end just yet . . .

*Chapter Seven*

## SOMETHING GOES WRONG

Peter had been sitting in Mr Latimer's office without saying anything much, although he was following the whole conversation very closely. At last he did ask a question of his own.

'On the television news yesterday, they said the saucer had been spotted in several different places, some of them hundreds of kilometres apart,' he said. 'How do you explain that, sir? I mean, if the saucer was going as slowly as you and that flight plan say?'

Mr Latimer smiled. 'A good question!' he said approvingly. 'The fact is, there are *several* flying saucers. Don't worry – Earth isn't really being invaded by Martians, or not just yet anyway!'

Peter had to admit to himself that he *did* feel a little relieved. So it wasn't a case of one flying saucer belonging to Futura Chocolate, and all the rest to extra-terrestrial beings from outer space – thank goodness for that!

'We launched ten in all, identical with the one you found,' Mr Latimer explained. 'And you're the first to have found the message hidden in the cargo of chocolate on board the saucers.'

'We were lucky, actually,' said Colin. 'The saucer damaged itself before coming down.'

'I should think it got caught in a tree, or a gust of wind blew it to the ground more roughly than it should have come down,' George guessed. 'Do you all remember that violent storm, the night before last?'

'That sounds a very likely explanation,' said Mr Latimer. 'Well, the heavens were certainly on the side of you children!' And he smiled at his own joke.

'What are you going to do about the other saucers?' asked Peter.

'They'll go on flying until their batteries are finally exhausted, which ought to be tomorrow, and then they'll come down for the last time. And this evening we shall release the truth about our stunt to radio and television – so then all listeners and viewers will get to hear about Futura, the chocolate of tomorrow! I bet you that there'll be a crowd of hopeful treasure-seekers out in the countryside tomorrow, all looking for the nine other saucers. Meanwhile, we're rushing stocks of our chocolate to all sweetshops and super-markets overnight. Tomorrow morning, everyone will be able to buy Futura, the chocolate of tomorrow – and as our slogan will add, "you can eat it today!" '

Mr Latimer was getting all enthusiastic about his chocolate. His cheeks were pink and his glasses were bouncing about on his nose as he talked excitedly. Scamper had gone to sleep, but now he woke and looked up in surprise.

'We decided to make this publicity campaign really big!' Mr Latimer went on. 'You see, we're entering the market in competition with a rival firm which already sells a great deal, and is one of the better-known brands – I mean Marvello Chocolate.'

'Ooh, yes, I've heard of Marvello Chocolate!' said Janet.

Mr Latimer didn't seem terribly pleased! He told her, 'You've heard of Marvello Chocolate *now*, but you'll soon forget all about it! There will be only *one* chocolate you or anyone else will want to buy: Futura, the chocolate of tomorrow – but you can eat it today!'

Goodness, thought Colin, he *is* keen on his firm's product! I wonder how many more times he's going to tell us that? 'By the way,' he said out loud, 'could you tell us what we've won?'

'Yes – yes, of course!' said Mr Latimer, getting his breath back. Obviously he was feeling he'd been a bit silly to let himself be so carried away. 'You children have won – ' And he paused for effect! 'Each and every one of you children has won – his or her weight in chocolate!'

'Great!' cried the delighted Pam.

'Hooray! Hooray!' shouted the others, clapping.

Suddenly, however, their shouts of joy were interrupted by the ringing of the telephone. Mr Latimer picked up the receiver.

'Hallo? Yes, this is the managing director of Futura Chocolate speaking . . . yes . . . yes, good morning, Chief Commissioner . . .'

The Seven pricked up their ears. He sounded as if he were talking to somebody *very* important!

'What? But that's impossible!' cried Mr Latimer. Then he listened to whoever it was at the other end of the line for quite a long time. He was looking very upset.

The children sitting in front of him exchanged enquiring glances. What was going on? Mr Latimer's voice was quite different now, and nothing like as enthusiastic as before. It was even trembling slightly.

'But how can it have happened?' he asked. 'I just don't understand!' He seemed to be on the defensive. 'I do assure you, Chief Commissioner, it can't possibly be anything for which *we* are responsible . . .'

What on earth had happened? The Seven waited impatiently for Mr Latimer to put the receiver down again. They were on tenterhooks!

At last the telephone conversation came to an end. 'Very well . . . yes, of course,' said Mr Latimer. 'Keep me up to date, will you? Thank you, Chief Commissioner.' And he rang off.

Eight pairs of eyes were fixed enquiringly on him.

'Well, talk about truth being stranger than fiction!' he said in a hollow voice. 'Apparently a rogue flying saucer is attacking towns and villages in this part of the countryside, causing panic wherever it goes and doing a great deal of damage. It's ploughed up lawns, broken branches off trees . . .' Poor Mr Latimer stopped, shaking his head. He was obviously shattered by the news.

'But you told us the flying saucers were quite safe!' said Peter. 'What you've heard sounds impossible! You said the saucers were designed and programmed to fly only over the open countryside!'

'Yes, and every word I said was true!' Mr Latimer assured the leader of the Seven. 'What's more, the *only* saucer launched in these parts is out of action, because it's the one you found yourselves. I just can't make it out. Now the police are accusing me of taking the joke too far. They think *I'm* responsible!'

He was too upset to say any more for a few moments. Then he rose, and pointed to the door with a trembling hand.

'Children, I'm very sorry indeed our conversation had to end like this,' he said. 'But I'm sure you'll understand when I say I need to be alone for a little while, to think what I can do about this terrible situation.'

'That's quite all right,' Peter's father told him, looking very sympathetic, and he shook hands with the managing director of Futura Chocolate. The Seven couldn't think of anything to say to the poor man – they just nodded goodbye to him, and a little later they were leaving the factory.

The sign-painters had finished their work, and Futura Chocolate had taken over from Black Cat Chocolate in front of the building. But now that this dreadful thing had happened, would Futura Chocolate itself last long?

Soon the van was on its way back to the village, with the Seven talking nineteen to the dozen inside as Peter's father drove them home.

'This time it really *must* be an extra-terrestrial invasion!' said Peter darkly.

'It's odd, all the same,' said Colin. 'Just think of *real* U.F.O.s arriving at the very moment when there are ten fake ones flying around!'

'That's why!' said Pam.

'What do you mean?' asked Barbara.

'Well, the Martians, or the extra-terrestrials or – well, the real creatures from space, whatever they are – they didn't like Futura Chocolate launching pretend flying saucers as a publicity stunt, so they decided to get their revenge.'

'Reprisals, that's the word you're looking for,' said Jack. 'Reprisals. And you could be right! I remember reading a science fiction book which said extra-terrestrials could see what was going on here on Earth from light-years away!'

The Seven felt very much impressed by what Jack said. There was a long silence. Poor little Janet was feeling dreadfully worried, and was glad her father was with them. She decided to appeal to *him*.

'Daddy – what do you think's happening?' she asked.

'Dear me, we'll have to wait and see, won't we?' he said gravely – but the Seven could tell at once he didn't believe in creatures from outer space, and Janet immediately felt better.

However, her father was not happy about this new twist to the tale of the flying saucers. He wasn't laughing as wholeheartedly as he had the night before, when Peter showed him the letter the Seven had found in the saucer among the brambles. There must be *something* rather unpleasant going on – but what? Well, he repeated to himself as he drove on, we'll have to wait and see!

He didn't know how right he was ... because twenty minutes later, when they were nearly back in the village, they *did* see!

The first houses were just in sight. Suddenly Peter and Janet's father trod hard on the brake. The tyres of the van squealed, and the Seven were thrown forward in the van and against each other.

When they straightened up, they saw an amazing sight through the windscreen.

They saw a flying saucer – a *real* flying saucer, huge and shiny, coming down over the village. As it passed, it left a great trail of orange vapour behind it.

Scamper, seeing this amazing vision, started barking for all he was worth.

The saucer came closer and closer to the houses, without slackening its speed at all. A moment later it had disappeared behind the rooftops. Pam instinctively put her hands over her ears, expecting an explosion. But nothing happened. Then, a few seconds afterwards, a cloud of smoke or vapour rose over the village. Rigid with shock, the Seven saw the flying saucer rise into the air again. It went up and up

into the sky, and soon it was just a little shiny dot. Then it disappeared entirely.

'What in the world. . . ?' breathed Peter and Janet's father. 'Or *out* of it!' he added.

'Oh, quick, Dad, let's go and see what's happened!' said Peter.

His father started the engine of the van again, put his foot on the accelerator, and drove fast all the way through the village. Then, suddenly, they all heard a shrill whistle somewhere overhead.

'It's coming back!' shrieked Janet.

Pressing their faces to the windows of the van, eyes wide with fear, the Seven saw the flying saucer coming down over the village again.

'What an awful noise!' said George, stopping his ears.

The saucer had reached the rooftops again by now.

'It's going to come down outside the Post Office!' cried Colin.

Peter's father swung his steering wheel round and began driving the way Colin was pointing, turning the van so suddenly that it went up on the pavement. Inside the van, the Seven clung to each other so as not to fall over again.

'Look at the vapour!' said Jack. There was a kind of faint mist rolling down the street ahead of them. But Peter's father wasn't going to stop for that. He drove the van straight into the orange mist, and a moment or so later he came out into the wide space by the village green, opposite the Post Office.

Then he stopped short. A stranger sight met his eyes than anything he could ever have imagined!

*Chapter Eight*

## MEN FROM OUTER SPACE

The flying saucer had come down in the middle of the village green. Thick misty vapour was billowing out of it — and strange beings were emerging from the saucer, walking through this mist. They had green skin and scarlet hair.

'Somebody wake me up!' Colin begged his friends, staggered.

But he wasn't dreaming! He looked again, taking in the whole amazing scene. The village green was in chaos. It stood where four roads met, and there was a certain amount of parking space — but several cars had run into each other. Those drivers who hadn't had time to get away had taken refuge underneath their own cars. There were several abandoned bicycles and motor scooters lying about, and one motor-bike. Packages and shopping bags and all sorts of other things had been dropped to the ground and left just where they were in the panic.

Suddenly the wind rose. The vapour drifted away, and the Seven could get a good view of the saucer. It was like a huge, shallow metallic cone, open at the top. Underneath the centre of it the children could clearly see a kind of folding ladder, let down to the ground.

There were four of the green men with scarlet hair. They moved like robots, with heavy, jerky steps.

Suddenly, as if telepathy united all four of them, they raised their arms at the same moment in a solemn gesture.

'I don't *believe* it!' George whispered, terrified.

Rays of light were coming from the ends of the creatures' fingers! It was a most alarming sight. Pam and Barbara couldn't bear to look – they hid their faces in their hands.

If the two girls had dared to go on looking a moment or so longer they would have seen another extraordinary thing – the four extra-terrestrials began flashing beams of light from their eyes as well!

Inside the van, Scamper suddenly went wild. He started bounding about all over the place, and nobody could stop him. In trying to catch hold of him, Janet fell off the seat and grazed her knee. Scamper growled, showing his teeth. Then he leaped up on the front seat, beside Peter and Janet's father, put both front paws on the door handle, gave a jump as he pushed down hard, and actually managed to get the door open.

'Scamper – come here!' Peter shouted after him, but Scamper wasn't listening to his young master. He was running for the flying saucer as fast as his paws would carry him.

Without a moment's hesitation, Peter jumped out of the van himself and rushed after the dog.

'Come back! Don't run such risks, you idiot – come back, Peter!' his father shouted.

But Peter took no notice. He just ran faster than before.

Scamper was a little way ahead of him. The dog disappeared into the cloud of vapour. When they saw him coming, the four extra-terrestrials turned back towards their saucer.

Peter had nearly caught up with them – but he was rooted to the spot by what happened next. It was all over so quickly! The whistling grew louder than ever, the whole of the village green was covered with vapour, and to everyone's amazement the flying saucer rose slowly from the ground again. It went up past the rooftops, straight into the sky, and disappeared in the distance.

There was total silence. And Peter realised what had happened. The flying saucer had gone again – taking his beloved Scamper with it!

'Scamper!' yelled Peter, looking up at the sky.

Next moment his six friends had joined him.

'They've kidnapped him!' cried Peter. 'Poor old Scamper! We'll never see him again.'

Janet burst into tears, and Pam and Barbara couldn't help crying either.

'They're crazy, whoever or whatever they are!' said Colin indignantly. 'Just look at the chaos they created!'

Life was trying to get back to normal on the village green. The drivers were looking to see how much damage had been done to their cars when they ran into each other. Cyclists were picking up their bicycles and shoppers were looking for the bags and baskets they had dropped. A mother was running about looking for her baby, and several children were crying. Everyone seemed to be shouting all at once.

Then the siren of a police car cut through the noise. The car stopped in the road by the village green, and the Inspector began trying to find out what had happened.

There was nothing the Seven could do. Very sadly, feeling too miserable even to utter a word, they went back to the van. Peter told his father how Scamper had been kidnapped. Stifling an exclamation, his father started the engine of the van again.

A few moments later, the Seven were driving away from the scene of this extraordinary incident.

If ever there had been a moment for an emergency meeting of the Secret Seven in Peter and Janet's garden shed, this was it! The children could hardly say a word, they were so shattered. For once they didn't even bother with the password. They just sat staring at the worn-out old rug on the floor of the shed. Scamper loved that rug. He often went to sleep on it if the Seven's meetings went on too long for his liking.

Janet couldn't stop crying. Pam and Barbara were sniffing at regular intervals, and kept blowing their noses on hankies already wet with tears.

After rather a long time, Colin got to his feet. 'Listen, we must pull ourselves together!' he said. 'After all, none of us actually *saw* Scamper get into the flying saucer, did we? There was too much vapour!'

'You're right,' George agreed. 'He may have escaped. He was beside himself with fury, remember.'

'And he could be wandering around the countryside at this very moment, hopelessly lost,' said Barbara.

'That *is* a possibility,' Peter agreed. 'On the other hand, it's just as likely he may be on board that saucer – and by now it's probably light-years away from Earth!'

'Woof!' said a familiar voice. 'Woof, woof!'

'*Scamper*!' cried Janet, rushing for the door. In a twinkling she had pulled back the bolt and was lifting the latch.

There was the spaniel sitting outside!

'Oh, *dear* old Scamper, you're back!' she said happily, through the tears she was still shedding. 'Back safe and sound! Oh, thank goodness!'

She hugged and patted the dog, making such a fuss of him that she didn't even notice a young man coming up to her.

'Good afternoon,' said the stranger. He seemed pleased to see the happy meeting between Janet and the dog.

Janet didn't even hear him! It was Peter who replied to the young man!

'Good afternoon,' he said, 'and thank you! Do come in and tell us how you found Scamper!'

The young man went into the shed, sat down, and introduced himself to the children. 'My name's Philip Belton,' he said, 'and I'm a student. Well, about twenty minutes ago I was driving along the Covelty road when I suddenly saw your dog rushing along towards me. I put the brakes on at once, and he immediately jumped up on the bonnet of my car, barking very loudly and looking imploringly at me through the windscreen. I realised he was asking me for a lift! And he's got his address on his collar, so it was easy for me to find his home!'

'That was most awfully kind of you,' said Jack. 'And it must have taken you a long way out of your way – if you were going to Covelty you'd have had to turn right round and drive back here in the opposite direction!'

'Oh, that doesn't matter a bit,' Philip Belton assured them. 'I've got plenty of time just now – it's the Easter vacation, you know. I expect you're on holiday from school yourselves!'

'How far away was Scamper when you found him?' asked Colin.

'He was near the old wishing well,' said the student.

'But that's nearly *in* Covelty!' said Barbara,

startled. 'It would take a dog ages to get there! How did he ever manage to run all that way in such a short time?'

'That's a good point, Barbara,' said George. 'If you picked him up twenty minutes ago, Mr Belton, and . . . let's see, it's an hour ago he vanished, isn't it?' he asked his friends.

'Just under,' said Jack, looking at his watch.

'Then he can only have taken half an hour to run from the village almost all the way to Covelty!' said George, amazed.

In fact, none of the Seven could make it out. It just wasn't possible for a golden spaniel to have run from the village to Covelty in that time! So how had he got to the place where Philip Belton picked him up? It was a mystery.

'Perhaps he hitched a lift going as well as coming back!' suggested Pam.

'I still think he was kidnapped by those extra-terrestrials!' said Peter.

'By *what*?' asked Philip Belton, smiling.

'By the extra-terrestrials,' Jack repeated, as if it were a perfectly ordinary explanation. 'They took him away in their flying saucer!'

'Don't you think you may have been reading a bit too much science fiction lately?' said the student, roaring with laughter.

'Oh, but the Earth's been invaded by U.F.O.s – didn't you know?' said Janet, still clutching Scamper. She hadn't let go of him since he turned up again.

'Why, no — I haven't so much as listened to the radio for a week,' said Philip. 'I've been camping with some friends, and I was just on my way to stay with one of them at his home when I met your dog.'

'Well, it's in all the papers,' said Peter. 'Hang on a moment, and I'll go and find one indoors. Then you'll see we're not just making it up!'

He hurried out of the shed and ran up the garden path. A moment later he was back, waving the front page of the local newspaper in front of the astonished young student.

'FLYING SAUCERS ATTACK OUR REGION!' Philip read out aloud. Then he ran his eye quickly down the four columns occupied by this sensational news story.

'Astounding!' he breathed, in blank surprise. 'Well, I'd really never have believed that —'

'That we were telling the truth?' Colin interrupted drily. 'You thought we were just a lot of silly kids trying to impress you, right?'

'Er — not exactly!' said Philip, sounding embarrassed. 'All the same . . .'

He stopped, feeling awkward about underestimating the Seven. Jack decided to put him at his ease by telling him the whole story from the very beginning — how the Seven and Susie and Binkie had seen the flying saucer by night, how they had met the five men on the hillside next day, and then how they had found the saucer after it had crash-landed, and discovered it was full of bars of chocolate.

At this point Barbara took over, and told Philip about their interview with the chairman and managing director of Futura Chocolate, and then how they came home to the village, filling in all the details of the flying saucer which was attacking it at the time.

Philip Belton was staggered. 'My word, what a lot of enterprise and energy you young people have put into this business!' he said. 'Er — if there's anything at all that I can do to help . . . ?'

'Oh yes, there is!' said Peter. 'You could drive us to the place where you found Scamper. Perhaps we'll find a trail to follow there! Because I'm beginning to think that this second flying saucer may not be any more of a *real* spacecraft than the first one was!'

And now that the other children had partly got over their fright, *they* were beginning to think the same as their leader!

Philip agreed to drive them along the Covelty road at once. The main problem was fitting eight people and a dog into his car, which was not a very big one! But the Seven all squashed up like sardines, and Janet held Scamper on her lap, and at last they set off, feeling very excited. What might they find when they reached the old wishing well?

*Chapter Nine*

## SCAMPER LEADS THE WAY

Twenty minutes later, just as the wishing well came in sight, Philip stopped his car a little way from a sharp bend in the road.

'Scamper came round that bend!' he told the children. 'And that's all I can tell you, really – he was running towards me, and he didn't tell me where he'd been!'

'Well, he'll tell *us*!' said Peter confidently. He got out, lifting the spaniel off his sister's lap, and put him down in the road. 'Come on, let's get down to work!' he told Scamper.

Scamper realised what Peter wanted him to do at once. He immediately began running on along the road in front of the car, barking, and turning round to look back now and then, as much as to ask the children why they weren't following him!

'On we go, then!' Peter told Philip Belton, and he got back into the car.

Once he heard the car's engine purring along behind him, the spaniel wagged his tail and ran faster. Philip kept a little distance in between them.

The dog and the car had gone on like this for ten minutes or so when Scamper suddenly stopped.

'Woof! Woof! Woof!' he barked.

Then he set off across country through the fields, turning round again as if inviting the others to follow him.

'Don't go so fast, Scamper!' Janet called. 'Hang on — we're coming!'

Philip parked the car by the side of the road, and soon they were all running after the spaniel.

They crossed fields, ran along beside a little river, and then went up a pebbly little path which ended on the outskirts of a large wood.

'Oh dear, it's private property!' said Barbara, disappointed. She had seen a notice on a tree-trunk.

'Well, there's no fence or anything,' said Pam. 'I don't see why we can't go on!'

'KEEP OUT. TRESPASSERS WILL BE PROSECUTED,' said George, reading the words of the notice. They were printed in white on a red background.

There was something else on the notice too, in smaller letters. 'I say!' Colin exclaimed, when he had read it.

'What's up?' asked Janet.

'Didn't you read the bottom line?' asked Colin. 'Look — the words are rather small, but they're legible!'

'Property of Marvello Holdings Ltd., London!' Philip Belton read out loud.

'Marvello Chocolate!' cried Jack. 'This is beginning to make sense at last!'

'Quick, Scamper!' Peter told his dog. 'Back on the trail!'

And they all set off again, following the spaniel into the middle of the wood. They had been walking for about ten minutes when Scamper suddenly stopped and stood very still, nose in the air, ears pricked up – as far as a golden spaniel *can* prick up his ears! He was listening hard and trying to pick up a scent.

'I'm sure we're there,' Peter whispered to the others.

'Oh, look at that – there's a clearing ahead of us!' Jack said, pointing. Sure enough, they could see a sunlit clearing through the trees.

'We'll go on, but cautiously,' Philip Belton suggested.

Luckily there was a thick carpet of moss on the floor of the wood at this point. The Seven and Philip made their way forward, darting from tree to tree so as to keep under cover of the tree-trunks. They made no noise at all as they reached the edge of the clearing.

'See that odd bush over there?' whispered Colin. 'It strikes me it's got a funny sort of look about it!'

Yes – it was more like a kind of scaffolding covered with leaves. It was quite tall, and stood right in the middle of the clearing.

'I wish we'd brought field-glasses,' sighed Barbara.

'Let's wait here for a while,' Philip Belton said.

'And if nothing seems to be stirring after fifteen minutes – well, then we'll think what to do next.'

Everyone thought this was a good idea, except for Scamper. He was getting quite excited. His breath was coming fast and his eyes were shining. There was no way the children could make *him* keep still! To be on the safe side, Peter slipped his lead on.

'Ssh!' he whispered in the dog's ear. 'We don't

want anyone to notice us, Scamper!'

And Scamper obediently lay down in the grass, to show he understood. The children lay down as well, and so did Philip Belton.

Minute followed minute, and no one so much as moved. Now and then Scamper turned his head to watch a butterfly go past – that was all.

Philip was looking at his watch. When the fifteen minutes were up, he signalled to Peter that the waiting time they'd agreed upon was over.

'Now what?' asked Jack, under his breath.

'I suggest throwing pebbles,' said Colin. 'If there *is* anyone watching this clearing they'll be bound to react then.'

'Good idea!' said Pam. 'But there's just one thing – take a look at the ground. No pebbles! At least, all *I* can see is moss.'

'Pine cones will do just as well,' said Peter, picking up a handful. And sure enough, there were pine cones lying all around.

Peter thought for a moment, and then handed his cones to Philip. 'You're the strongest of us,' he said, 'and probably the best shot too!'

'I'm not so sure about that!' said the student, who was much impressed by the Seven! 'But I'm happy to try, if you like.'

He leaped to his feet, swung back his arm, and threw the first pine cone as hard as he could.

It hit the enormous bush with a loud metallic 'clang'.

'Well,' said Colin, grinning, 'unless that's a very rare species of metal shrub, I'm ready to bet there's something hidden underneath the leaves.'

'Let's go and look!' said Jack.

He was getting to his feet, but Peter held him back.

'Take it easy!' Peter whispered. 'Wait a minute, Jack!'

'I'll have another go,' Philip said. 'You never know – and we may only have imagined what we heard the first time.'

So he threw three more pine cones – and each time they hit the 'bush' with the same metallic sound.

There was no other reaction, though. Nothing moved.

The Seven and Philip waited just a moment longer, holding their breath. Then, at last, Peter said, 'Right – here goes!'

'Hang on – better not keep all together,' said George. 'Supposing we *were* attacked, there's a better chance of one at least escaping if we spread out.'

So spread out they did, all around the clearing. Scamper was let off his lead, and then they walked forward quite openly, going slowly and keeping very much on the alert.

Philip was the first to reach the bush. 'And it *isn't* a bush,' he said. 'Just as we thought! It's something camouflaged by netting with leaves over it.'

The Seven hurried to join him, and a moment later Peter and Jack were removing the camouflage of leaves. How surprised they all were when they saw the flying saucer standing there before them!

'I don't believe it!' cried Pam, in amazement.

'Look – the steps are down!' said Colin, pointing to the four folding steps. Sure enough, they were let down to the ground.

'I'm going in!' said Peter. 'I want to know what's inside!'

'Oh, Peter, don't!' Janet begged him. 'It's far too dangerous!'

She was so scared for her brother that she was almost in tears.

'Don't worry, Janet, I'll go with him,' Jack told her.

'No,' said Philip Belton firmly, 'Peter and I will go. The rest of you stay here – and if there's anything to alarm you at all, let us know by whistling through your fingers!'

'All right,' said George. 'But do be quick about it!'

Peter and Philip climbed the four steps leading to the inside of the flying saucer. But as they were about to go inside they stopped short. Neither of them could help uttering a cry of amazement!

'Good heavens!' said Philip.

'My *word*!' cried Peter.

They were astonished by the sight that met their eyes.

*The flying saucer was not a flying saucer at all!*

## Chapter Ten

## THE FLYING SAUCER EXPLAINED!

Peter and Philip were looking at a cleverly disguised helicopter – and *not* a spacecraft from somewhere light-years away from Earth!

'Here, come and take a look at this, everyone!' Peter called. 'It's all right! There's no danger of finding ourselves on another planet!'

The rest of the Seven came running up to join him. They all cried out in surprise – and when their first astonishment was over, they tried to work out just how the trick had been played.

When they looked more closely, they found that it was really very simple. The helicopter had been cleverly hidden inside a large, flattened metal cone. You couldn't see it at all from outside the cone, so that the whole contraption really did look like everyone's idea of a flying saucer. And letting off coloured smoke bombs must have helped!

Now that they knew what it really was, Jack and George made their way inside the helicopter. The others, still outside, heard them burst out laughing – and a moment later two green faces crowned by mops of scarlet hair looked out of the toughened glass dome of the helicopter at them!

Janet was so scared she nearly fainted. But it was only George and Jack, in the masks worn by the 'extra-terrestrials'. The two boys came out and showed their friends the rubber costumes they had found inside, too. There were little mirrors glued to the ends of the fingers of the costumes, and above each eye of the masks.

'I suppose the mirrors just reflected the sun, and that was all!' said Barbara. 'And to think we took them for death rays or something!'

Jack and Colin went back to finish their search of the helicopter – and when they came out again they weren't laughing any more.

'We've just been looking at their plan of action – it's all written down on a piece of paper stuck up near the controls,' said Colin.

'The next place they're going to is Castleford,' said George. 'And the attack's planned for five o'clock this afternoon.'

'It's nearly two now,' said Philip, glancing at his watch. 'I suppose your friends from outer space have gone to have lunch. We'd better get a move on before they come back.'

'Marvello Chocolate – of course! I might have guessed it!' Colin suddenly shouted. He had been exploring the underneath of the helicopter. 'This aircraft belongs to Marvello Holdings, just like the wood it's standing in!'

'How do you know?' asked Janet.

'It says so, on a little metal plate underneath the helicopter!'

'What a mean trick to play!' said Barbara. She could hardly get over it!

'Yes — the Marvello Chocolate people turned this helicopter into a flying saucer just to discredit Futura Chocolate's publicity campaign!' said Colin.

'Oh, I see!' cried Janet. 'Yes — they only needed to take the flying saucer game a little too far! That was supposed to be a joke — but they could have made it look dangerous and unpleasant.'

'And then nobody would have wanted to eat the "chocolate of tomorrow",' said Pam.

'They nearly *did* do a lot of damage, as well,' said Jack.

'They *have* done a good deal of damage already, in a way,' said Peter. 'I mean, Futura Chocolate won't be very popular anywhere the rogue flying saucer's already been, will it!'

'I call it a really underhand trick!' said George. 'Marvello Chocolate planned to sabotage their rivals before the public had even had a chance to try the Futura product! I don't call that fair.'

'Well, the game's not over yet,' said Colin. 'I've just thought of an idea which might make Marvello Chocolate laugh on the other side of its face!'

And *he* burst out laughing, much to his friends' surprise.

Two and a half hours later the Seven arrived in Castleford. Philip had very kindly driven them there in his car. They had made some telephone calls earlier – and they went straight to the biggest park in the town, where they met the Mayor, the Superintendent of Police, and Mr Latimer, the managing director of Futura Chocolate.

A little later, Susie and Binkie joined them, along with Peter and Janet's parents. The two little nuisances were still a bit pale, but they had recovered from their indigestion.

Several people, recognising the Mayor, came up and hung around out of curiosity. What could all these people be waiting for? Was some important person about to arrive in Castleford?

'This is going to be fun!' said Colin grimly. And he glanced at their helpful ally Philip Belton.

'You're sure this is where they're planning to land?' asked the Mayor of Castleford. He sounded anxious.

Peter *was* sure. He knew this park, and it was obviously the ideal place for the helicopter.

Suddenly they heard the noise of an aircraft engine up in the sky. Yes, it was just on five o'clock!

The Mayor and the Superintendent walked forward, and the crowd which had gathered fell silent.

A moment later a huge flying saucer appeared in the sky. It was shining in the sunlight. All the people went 'Ooh!' with surprise.

Once it was closer, the crowd could see a long publicity streamer flying out in its wake.

Colin was red in the face with his efforts not to laugh.

The flying saucer came closer still – and now everyone could read what the streamer said:

'IF YOU WANT A STOMACH-ACHE, EAT MARVELLO CHOCOLATE!'

Mr Latimer stood there staring. Colin was doubled up with laughter!

It had been his idea to use an old publicity streamer he had found in the bottom of the helicopter, writing new words on it and fastening it to the aircraft so that nobody inside would notice it was there when they took off.

Now the crowd were laughing like anything too. And when the fake U.F.O. began letting off coloured smoke bombs, everyone in the park applauded.

'As good as a Bank Holiday show!' said one enthusiastic spectator.

The 'saucer' came slowly down and landed in the middle of the park.

'What a racket it makes!' said the Police Superintendent. 'Sounds a bit like –'

'A helicopter!' said Pam, smiling.

'I'm afraid the extra-terrestrials' siren isn't working,' George gasped, in between roars of laughter. 'We did *help* it not to work,' he added.

At that moment the folding steps were let down.

'It's one of the Royal Family!' said a lady in the

crowd, hopefully.

But it wasn't one of the Royal Family. Four rather miserable-looking extra-terrestrials climbed out instead. They raised their arms in the air, moved their green faces desperately this way and that – no luck! They weren't producing any rays of light at all, because the sun had just gone behind dark clouds. Even the sky seemed to be on the side of the Seven just now.

The Police Superintendent put an end to the show by blowing his whistle – and immediately fifty policemen came running into the park and surrounded the helicopter. In no time at all, the 'extra-terrestrials' were in police custody.

When the policemen took off their masks, the crowd uttered cries of amazement. And so did the Seven.

'Those are four of the men who chased us off the hillside!' said Barbara.

'And there's the fifth!' said Jack. 'He was piloting the helicopter.'

'Aren't you bright!' said Susie, teasing her brother, but he only gave her a cross look.

'Well done, the Secret Seven!' said Mr Latimer cheerfully. He was looking very much happier than he had been when last they saw him. 'How can I ever thank you?' He frowned thoughtfully, adjusted his glasses, scratched his head, and then he had an idea. 'What about chocolate for life, for all of you?' he suggested.

'Woof!' said Scamper happily. 'Woof, woof, woof!'

Let's hope the Seven have more sense than Susie and Binkie, and don't give themselves indigestion. But they won't – because that might mean they would miss the chance of more adventures . . .